W9-DDJ-985

DISCARD

Wakarusa Public Library

SUPER DC HEROES
VILLAINS

SINESTRO
AND THE RING OF FEAR

WRITTEN BY
LAURIE S. SUTTON

ILLUSTRATED BY
SHAWN McMANUS
LEE LOUGHRIDGE

STONE ARCH BOOKS
a capstone imprint

Published by Stone Arch Books in 2012
A Capstone Imprint
1710 Roe Crest Drive
North Mankato, MN 56003
www.capstonepub.com

Copyright © 2012 DC Comics.
SINESTRO and all related characters and
elements are trademarks of and © DC Comics.
(s12)

STAR25084

No part of this publication may be reproduced
in whole or in part, or stored in a retrieval
system, or transmitted in any form or
by any means, electronic, mechanical,
photocopying, recording, or otherwise,
without written permission.

Cataloging-in-Publication Data is available at
the Library of Congress website

ISBN: 978-1-4342-3798-9 (library binding)
ISBN: 978-1-4342-3899-3 (paperback)

Summary: Leader of the Yellow Lantern
Corps, Thaal Sinestro, plans to control the
universe through fear. With his power ring,
the sinister super-villain travels from planet
to planet, terrorizing innocent citizens with
nightmarish creations. Luckily, Hal Jordan,
Guardian of the Universe, is out to stop
him. Will the Green Lantern prevail, or will his
former mentor scare Hal to death?

Printed in the United States of America in Stevens Point,
Wisconsin.
102011
006404WZS12

TABLE OF CONTENTS

SINESTRO

REAL NAME:
Sinestro

OCCUPATION:
Yellow Lantern

HEIGHT: 6' 7"

WEIGHT: 205 lbs.

EYES: Black

HAIR: Black

BIOGRAPHY:

Born on the planet Korugar, Thaal Sinestro was appointed the Green Lantern of Sector 1417 at an early age. Soon, he became one of the most powerful members of the entire corps. He mentored many rookie members of the Green Lanterns, including Hal Jordan of Earth. Although effective, his strict leadership style and fiendish imagination drew criticism. Unwilling to change, Sinestro's loyalty to the green power ring soon turned to hatred. He eventually left the Green Lanterns, donned a yellow ring, and formed his own Sinestro Corps.

Superior Intelligence

Yellow Power Ring

Fearsome Strength

High-tech Uniform

POWERS/ABILITIES:
Brilliant military
commander; ring creates
hard-light constructs
of anything imaginable;
unmatched power.

THE HIGHLORD OF QWARD

Everything has an opposite: light and dark, good and evil, positive and negative. The universe has an opposite, too — a place where evil is praised. A place where fear reigns. At the center of this negative universe is the planet Qward. It is a world of conquerors, warriors, and slaves. This is where the super-villain Sinestro rules.

Years ago, Sinestro was a powerful Green Lantern. He lived in the positive universe, but was banished by the Corps to the negative universe for a series of crimes.

He fit right in.

Sinestro teamed up with the Weaponers of Qward. They built all sorts of powerful technology including the yellow power rings of fear. Their goal was to conquer the positive universe. This was Sinestro's goal, too. The Green Lantern Corps lived in the positive universe, and he wanted revenge.

One day, Sinestro marched into the Throne Room of Qward. The Council of Commanders was gathered there. He had called them to hear an announcement. No one knew what he was going to say.

Sinestro stepped up to the throne. "Weaponers of Qward!" he said. "You have been my allies since I first came to this world."

The Council murmured in agreement.

"Thunderers," Sinestro continued, "you are the mightiest warriors in this universe!"

The Thunderers nodded their heads. No one disagreed with that statement.

"You are failures!" Sinestro declared.

Everyone in the room started shouting. They were angry with Sinestro for saying such a thing.

"You have failed in your goal to conquer the positive universe!" Sinestro said. "Do you deny it?"

The crowd shouted louder. It made them angry to remember their defeats at the hands of the Green Lantern Corps.

"I don't blame you for your failures," Sinestro said. "I blame a lack of proper leadership."

The commanders stopped yelling at Sinestro and looked at the Weaponlord and the Thunderlord instead. The two supreme leaders looked very uneasy.

"That's why I'm declaring myself the Highlord of Qward!" Sinestro said.

No one spoke or made a sound. They were too shocked by this announcement.

Sinestro walked over to the giant throne and sat down.

"There hasn't been a Highlord for generations," the Weaponlord said to the super-villain.

"That's the problem," Sinestro replied. "The Thunderers and Weaponers haven't been united — until now."

"But why should it be you?" the Thunderlord asked.

Sinestro smiled an evil grin and held up his fist. The yellow power ring flashed on his finger. The ring was one of the most dangerous weapons in any universe. "Are you challenging me?" Sinestro asked the Thunderlord.

The supreme commander of the Thunderer warriors glared at Sinestro. "A Thunderer never runs from a challenge!" he shouted.

A yellow beam shot from Sinestro's power ring, striking the Thunderlord in the chest. The warrior was thrown backward across the Throne Room. He crashed into a dozen other warriors before he hit a stone wall. The Thunderlord did not move. The armor on his chest smoldered from the yellow energy beam.

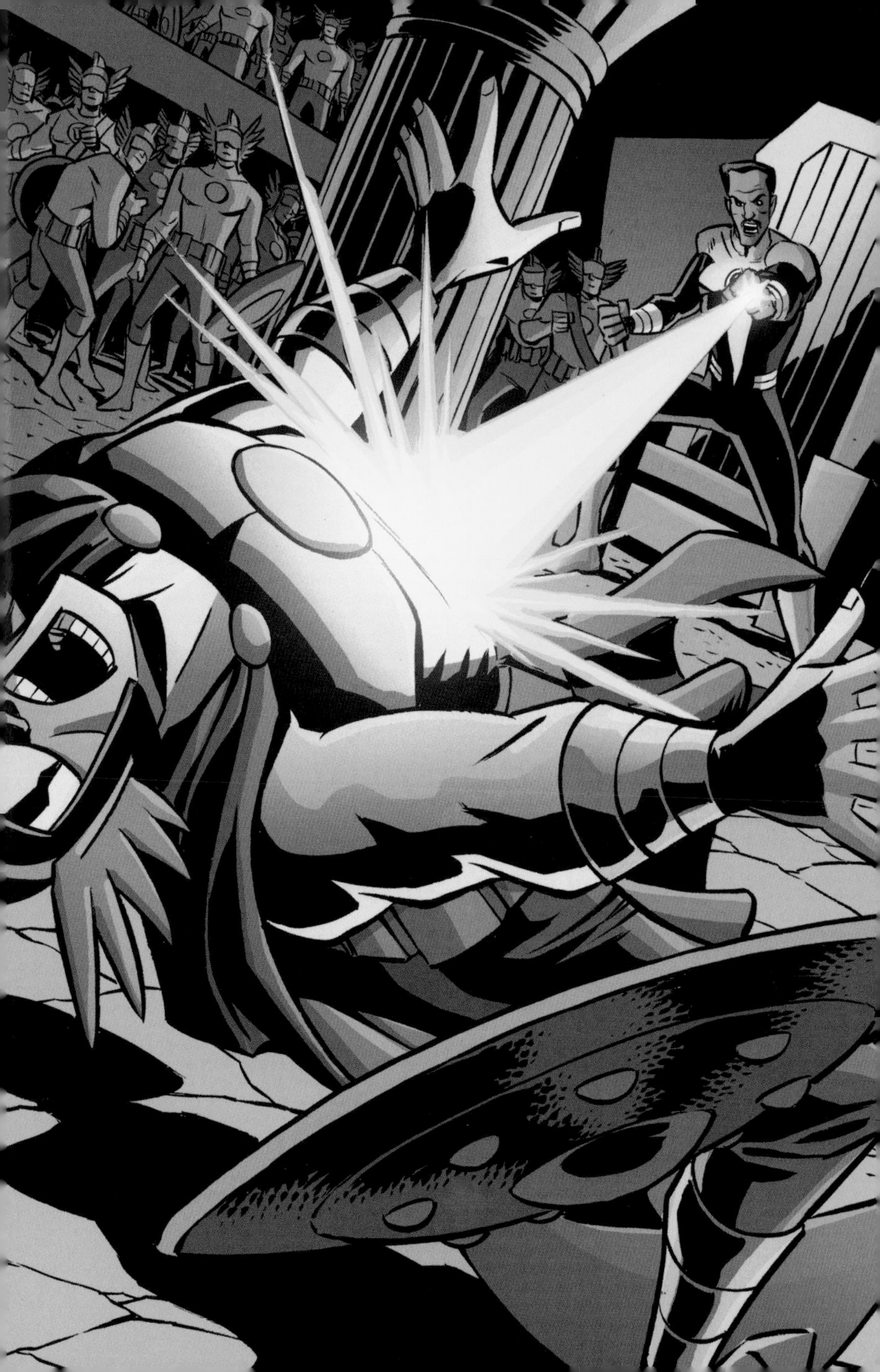

Sinestro looked triumphant.

"Is that all you've got?" the Thunderlord said, staggering to his feet.

Sinestro's power ring glowed, and the yellow energy formed a giant sword at his command. The blade zoomed toward the Thunderlord.

The warrior blocked the energy blade with his shield. Then he pulled a Qwa-bolt from his quiver and threw it at his opponent. The energy lance sizzled as it sped toward its target. Sinestro dodged just in time. The Qwa-bolt hit the top of the throne, and it exploded into fragments.

Sinestro willed the power ring to create a giant war hammer.

He pounded on the Thunderlord's shield. The Weaponers of Qward had made the shield. Nothing could harm it.

The supreme commander of the Thunderers threw a storm of Qwa-bolts at his foe. Sinestro formed a yellow force field and blocked the attack. Even so, the Thunderlord advanced toward him. The warrior was persistent.

"I'm impressed," Sinestro said. Then he willed his ring to form a cage around the warrior. "That's why I'm not going to destroy you."

The Thunderlord rammed his shield against the yellow bars. He hit them with Qwa-bolts, but the cage did not break.

"You are defeated. Accept me as Highlord," Sinestro said.

"I am the Thunderlord of Qward!" the warrior declared defiantly. He glared at Sinestro. "And I accept Sinestro as Highlord."

The cage dissolved around the Thunderlord. He dropped to his knees and stayed there.

"That's better," Sinestro said.

Sinestro went back to the Throne of Qward. It was half destroyed from the battle, but he sat on it as if it were whole.

"Now, let me show you how we're going to conquer the positive universe," he said, "and all the Green Lanterns in it!"

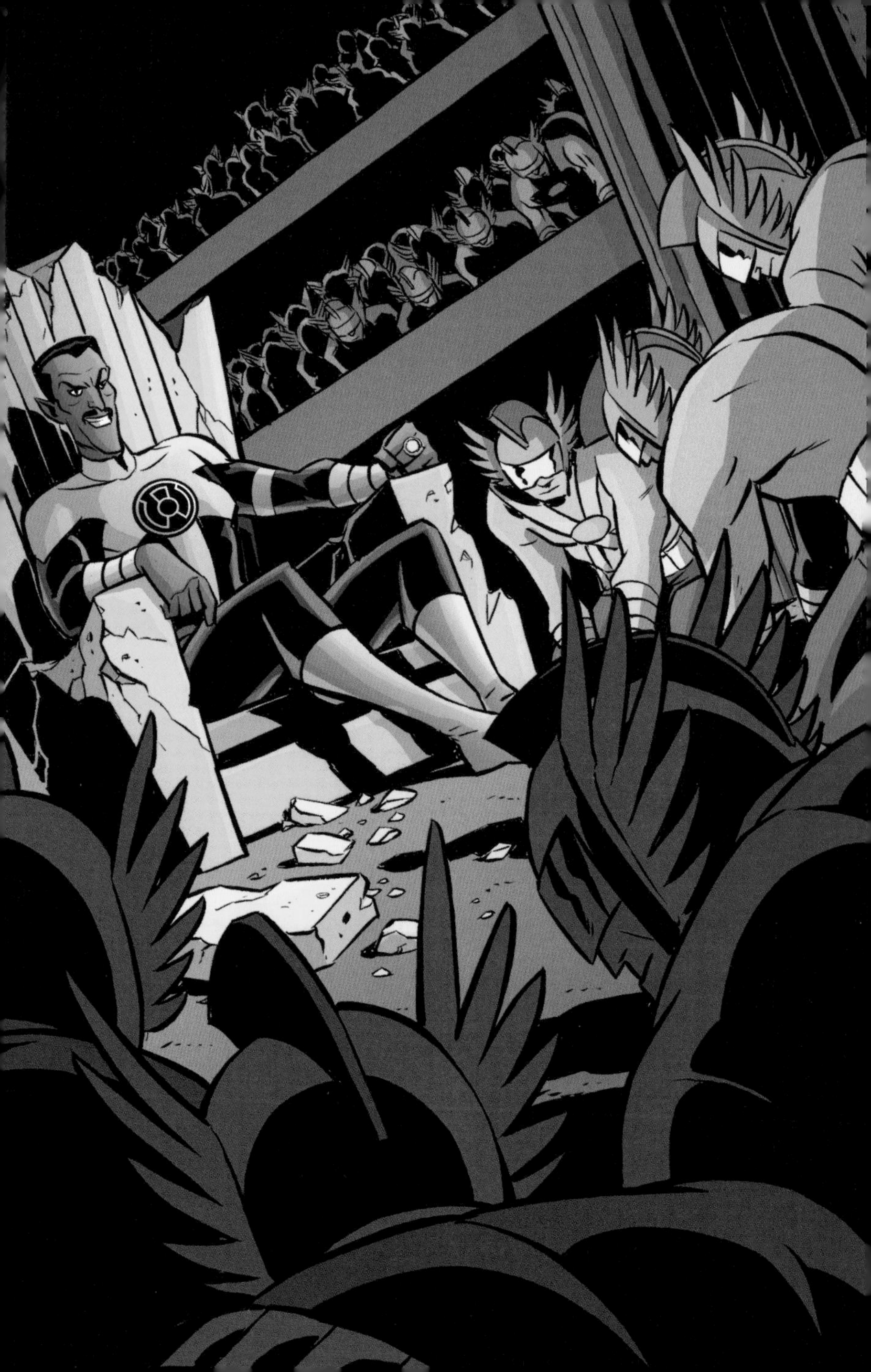

CHAPTER 2

RING OF FEAR

Sinestro sat on the Throne of Qward as Highlord. The population of the planet was his to command. "Weaponers! Bring in the Ring of Fear!" he ordered.

Twelve Qwardians marched into the Throne Room. Each of them carried a large metal box. They placed the boxes on the floor in a circle at the feet of their new Highlord.

"Behold the doom of the positive universe!" Sinestro declared.

The gathered commanders stared at the devices. No one spoke. Some of the Thunderers scratched their heads. Even the supreme Weaponlord appeared dumbfounded.

"It's a Qwa-Portal!" Sinestro revealed as if the fact was obvious.

"That's nothing new," the Thunderlord said, adjusting his dented armor. "It's a gateway between our universe and the other one. So what?"

"This one is different," Sinestro said. "This one is a super-portal designed to transport the entire planet of Qward into the positive universe!"

The Thunderlord pushed one of the boxes with his boot. He did not look convinced.

"I will take these components into the positive universe and activate them," Sinestro said. "Qward and all its inhabitants will be transported together. Then we will launch an invasion!"

"Invasion! The sound of that word is music to my ears!" the Thunderlord said.

"Thunderers! Weaponers! Make ready for war!" Sinestro shouted.

A loud cheer went up from everyone in the Throne Room. Sinestro pointed his power ring at the metal boxes and a beam of yellow energy surrounded them. They rose into the air. Sinestro floated in the middle of them. Then suddenly, there was a bright flash of yellow light.

Sinestro and the boxes vanished!

Seconds later, Sinestro appeared in the positive universe. The metal boxes hovered around him in a circle. He was in deep space, far away from any planets. This was just what he wanted.

Sinestro quickly went to work. He used the power ring to arrange the boxes in a giant circle as wide as a planet. It had to be big enough for Qward to fit through.

When that was done, Sinestro fired a beam of yellow energy at the nearest box.

The box popped open and released thousands of small golden metal globes. They began to line up like beads on a string. Sinestro flew ahead of them until they arrived at the next metal box.

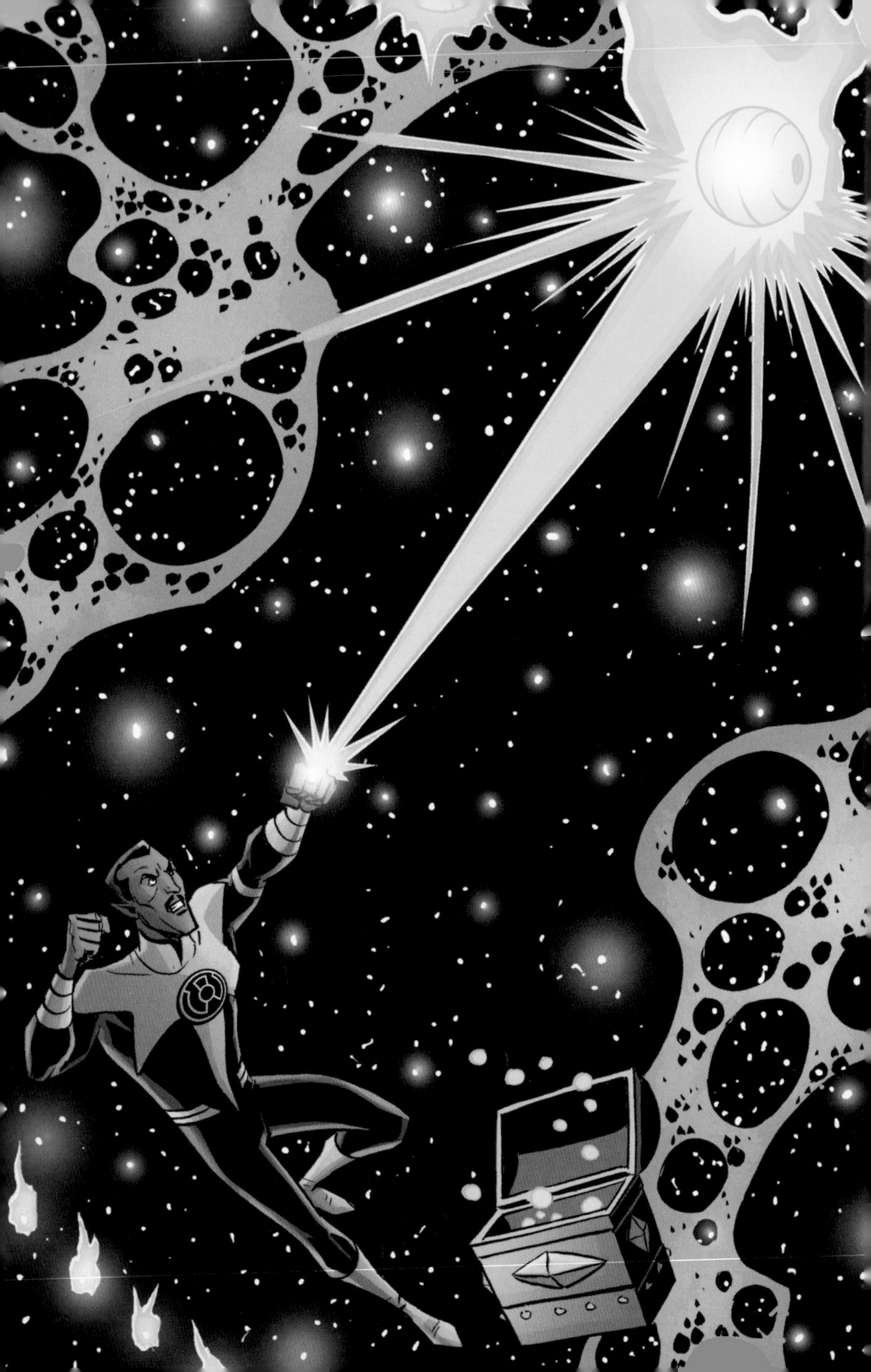

WHOOOOSH!

Another burst of power from his ring opened the box, and more globes were released. They lined up with the next box. This was repeated until a single enormous ring was formed.

"Phase one is complete," Sinestro said. "Now all I have to do is power up the portal with fear energy."

Sinestro commanded his ring to show him a map of the space sector. A chart appeared in front of him, which showed several stars and planets marked on a grid. Sinestro tapped the image of one planet with his finger. He smiled an evil smile.

"This little world is perfect," he said. "Its people are easy to terrorize. They'll generate plenty of fear energy."

Sinestro set off through space toward his goal. It didn't take him long to arrive at the planet. Sinestro used his power ring to form giant propeller blades to stir up the oceans.

Huge tidal waves crashed onto the land. The people on the planet were terrified. Sinestro transmitted their fear energy to the globes of the space ring.

Then suddenly, giant green dams blocked the waves from hitting the shorelines. Enormous green spheres formed around the propellers.

"Ha! A Green Lantern has come to the rescue," Sinestro observed. "I wonder which one . . ."

A moment later, the super-villain had his answer.

An alien in a Green Lantern uniform confronted Sinestro. It had a spherical head and many tentacles. A green ring glowed at the end of one of them.

"Sinestro!" the Green Lantern said. "You're back to cause more trouble, I see."

"Hello, Brokk," Sinestro replied with false courtesy. "I see you're still patrolling Sector 0981."

"Yes," said Brokk. "I haven't abandoned my duty to the Corps. Not like you."

"Being a Green Lantern got boring," Sinestro said with a laugh. "I went on to bigger and better things. I'm the Highlord of Qward now!"

"So why aren't you on Qward, Your Highness?" Brokk asked. "Did your subjects banish you?"

The words stung Sinestro. The Green Lantern Corps had banished him years ago, and the memory burned like a hot coal.

His mind commanded the yellow power ring. A beam of savage yellow energy shot from the ring and hit Brokk.

KA-BOOMMM!

The Green Lantern of Sector 0981 was protected from the vacuum of space by a green energy shield. The shield also saved him from Sinestro's sudden power blast. Brokk was thrown back toward the planet. He hit the atmosphere and didn't stop until he splashed into one of the oceans.

By the time Brokk recovered and flew back into space, Sinestro was gone.

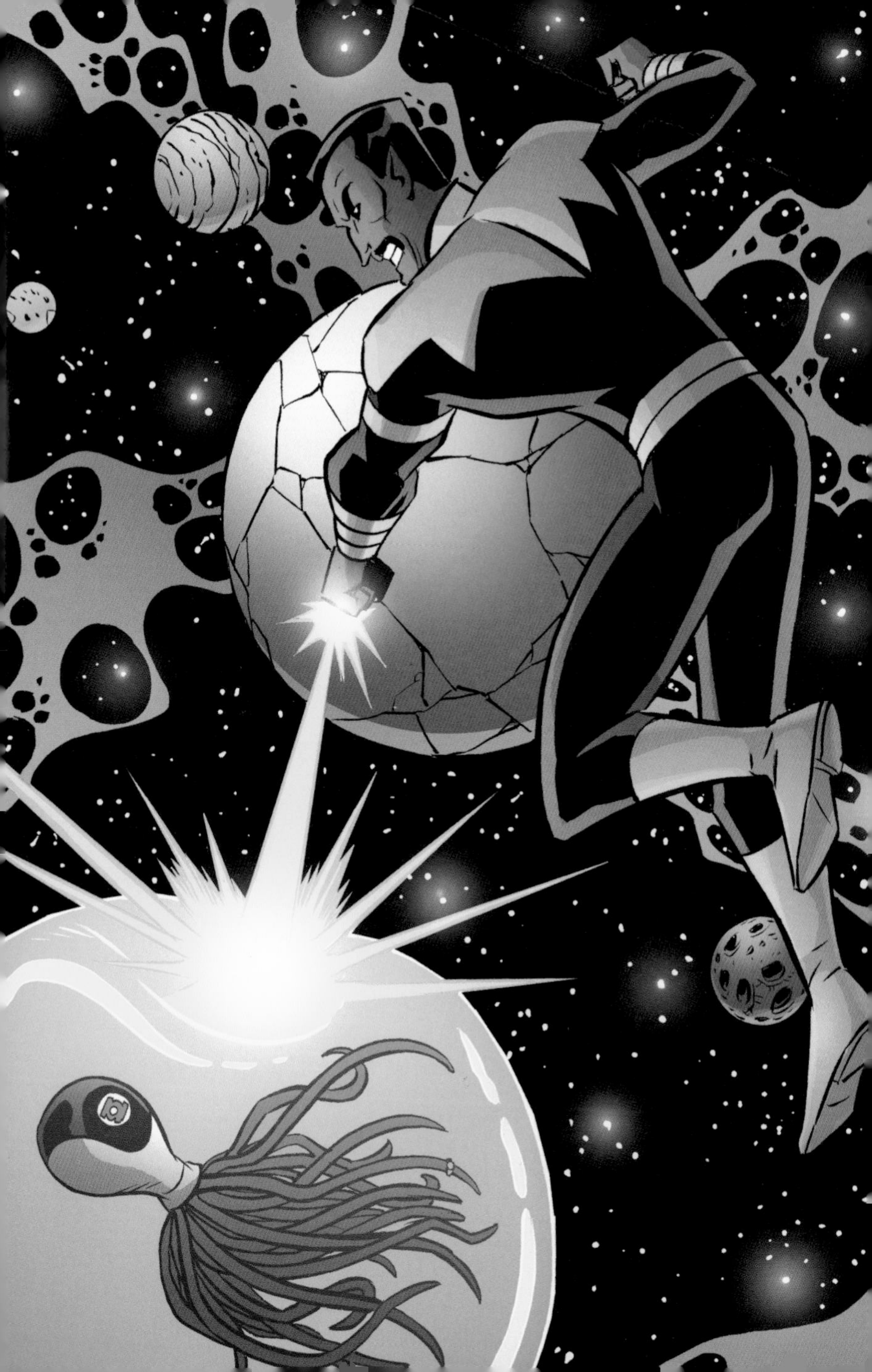

CHAPTER 3

THE SINESTRO CORPS

Sinestro floated near his Ring of Fear. One segment was lit up from the fear energy, but it wasn't enough power to bring Qward into the positive universe.

"It's going to take too long to feed fear into the ring one planet at a time," Sinestro realized. "I need to create terror on a massive scale."

The super-villain knew exactly how to do that. Sinestro held up his yellow power ring and used it to send out a message.

"Attention Sinestro Corps!" he said. "I command you to come to me! Come now!"

The villainous Corps members appeared just after Sinestro finished his message. The first to arrive was a giant humanoid with a mouthful of fangs and skin the color of an old bruise.

"Hello, Arkillo," Sinestro said.

The giant nodded but did not speak. He had lost his tongue in a fight.

Next came a creature that looked like a stingray. The barbs on its tails were deadly.

"Ah, Flayt, very prompt," Sinestro greeted the being.

Then Sirket arrived. He looked like a spider with sharp, pointy legs. Then came DevilDog. His body looked human but he also had horns and tusks and claws.

Next to him was Slushh. His whole body was liquid acid. The bones of his victims floated inside of him.

More and more members appeared. They came in every shape and size and species, but they had one thing in common. They all wore the black and yellow uniform of the Sinestro Corps.

"You were chosen to wear the yellow power ring because you are feared throughout the universe," Sinestro said to them. "Arkillo, your brutality is legendary. DevilDog, your evil has never been matched. I need those talents today."

The gathered aliens cheered. They were always willing to spread massive amounts of mayhem. "I need the fear energy from many worlds to energize my Ring of Fear," Sinestro said.

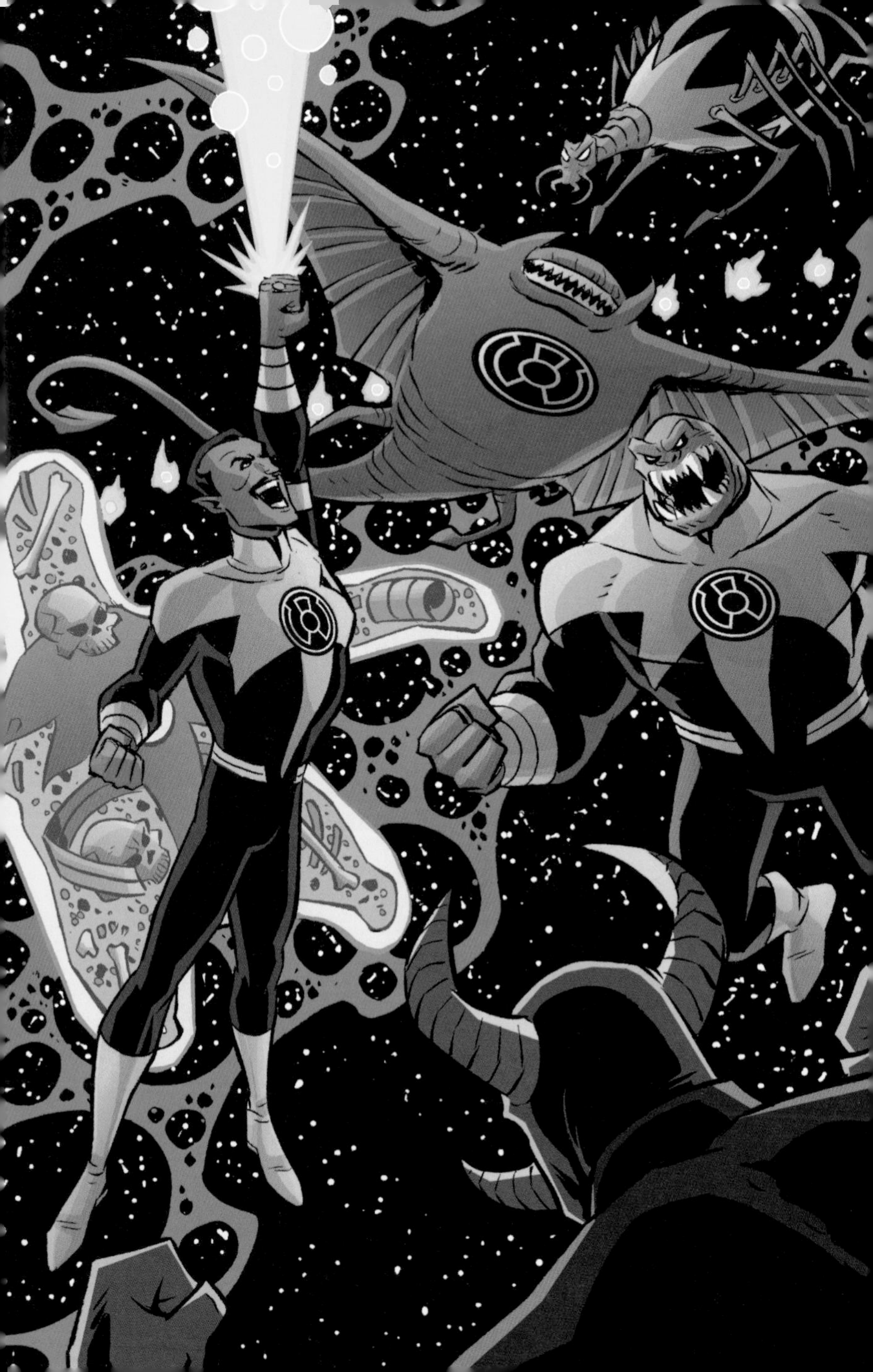

He used his power ring to make small mechanical discs and attached them to their uniforms.

"These transmitters will collect the fear energy and send it to the Ring of Fear," Sinestro explained. "Now go and make the universe tremble in terror!"

The Sinestro Corps members flew off in every direction. Sinestro didn't care where they went, as long as they did not enter Sector 2814. He claimed that sector for himself. That's where the planet Earth was located — the homeworld of his old enemy, Hal Jordan.

When Sinestro arrived at Earth, he sent a swarm of yellow energy missiles at the tiny blue planet.

They exploded near New York and
Tokyo and London. Sinestro did not want to
destroy the cities. Not yet. First, he wanted
the people to feel fear.

The missiles were not enough for
Sinestro. He imagined monsters. His ring
created the scariest creatures in the universe
and sent them down to Earth. He smiled
an evil smile. Now the people were really
starting to scream.

Suddenly, a giant green fist punched the
super-villain. He was knocked halfway to
the moon. Only one person could do that
to him.

"Sinestro, leave my world alone!" said
Hal Jordan, the Green Lantern of Earth.

"I'm just getting started," Sinestro said.

The super-villain created a tremendous pump that started sucking the water from the Atlantic Ocean. It sprayed out into space and froze solid. Soon, there were icebergs floating in orbit.

"That's just a warm up," he said. "How do Earthlings feel about the dark? You're not afraid of it, are you?"

Hal didn't give Sinestro a chance to put his evil words into action.

He blasted his enemy with a beam of green energy that sent Sinestro out of the solar system.

"This is just the beginning!" Sinestro taunted as he disappeared.

"The beginning of what?" Hal wondered aloud. "That doesn't sound good."

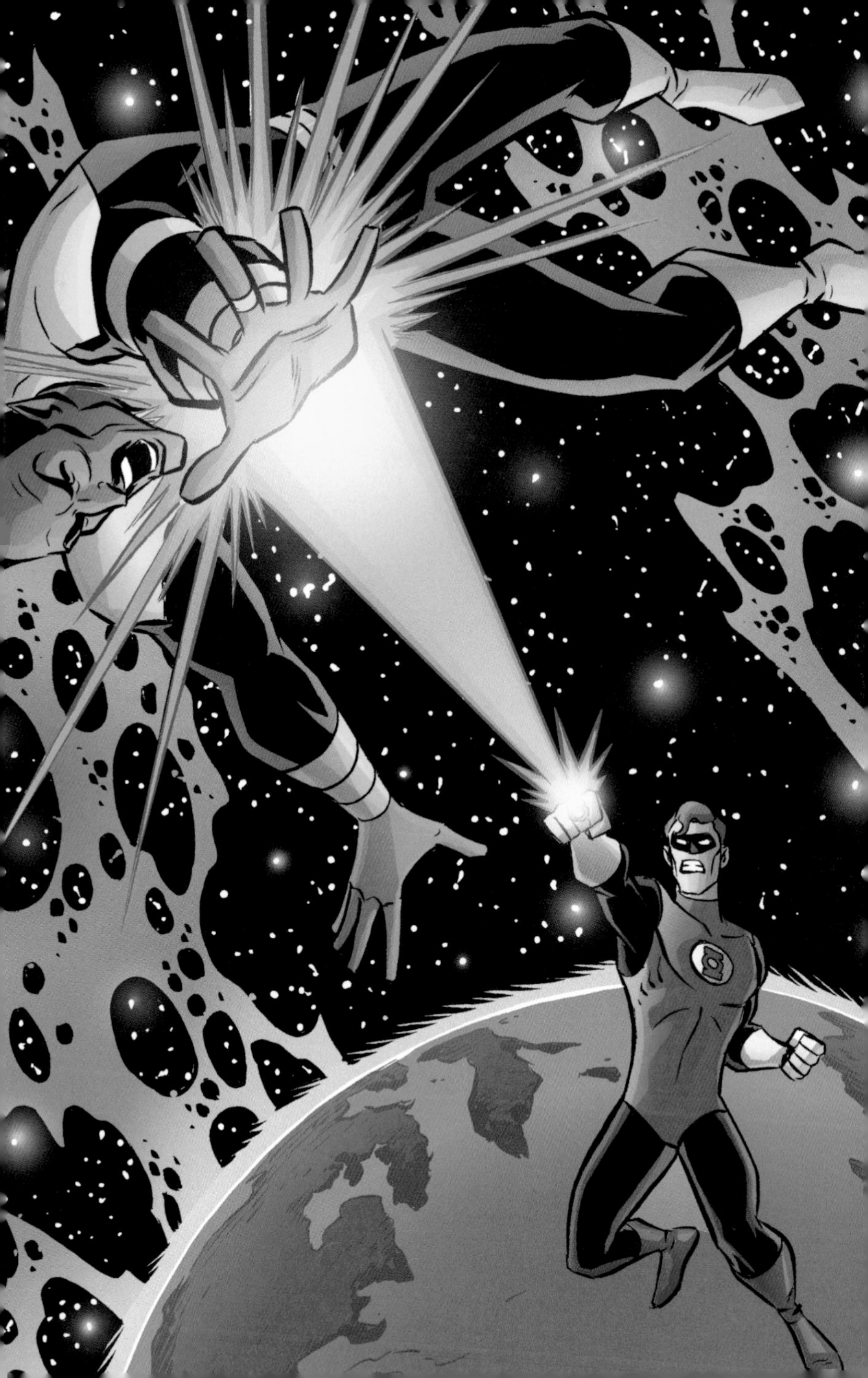

Hal flew off in pursuit of Sinestro. The super hero couldn't let his enemy escape. He had to find out what Sinestro was planning.

"Attention Green Lantern Corps," Hal said. His ring transmitted the message across the galaxy and beyond. "Sinestro is back in our universe. He must be captured. Be on the lookout and report."

"Green Lantern of Earth," came a reply. "This is Brokk of Sector 0981. I battled Sinestro a short time ago."

"I'm chasing him right now," Hal said. "Home in on my signal, and we'll team up. Sinestro is up to something BIG!"

CHAPTER 4

SCARE TACTICS

Sinestro returned to the Ring of Fear. Four sections out of twelve were now lit up. Sinestro had expected more. Many Sinestro Corps members were out spreading fear.

Why isn't the entire Ring powered up by now? Sinestro wondered.

"DevilDog, report!" the super-villain said into his power ring.

"Mission going as planned," DevilDog replied. "Three planets down and plenty more to go. This is fun!"

DevilDog's laugh was almost as evil as Sinestro's. He enjoyed terrorizing people. Right now, he was chasing the crab people of an aquatic world with giant yellow hammers created by his power ring.

SMASH! They scattered in fear.

"It's not enough!" Sinestro said. "The Ring needs more fear energy. Increase your terror levels!"

"You asked for it, you got it," DevilDog replied.

DevilDog formed a tremendous yellow energy net and scooped up thousands of crab people. They waved their little legs and claws, trying to escape. Their tiny voices screamed. DevilDog held the net over the top of a volcano. The threat of the bubbling lava intensified their fear.

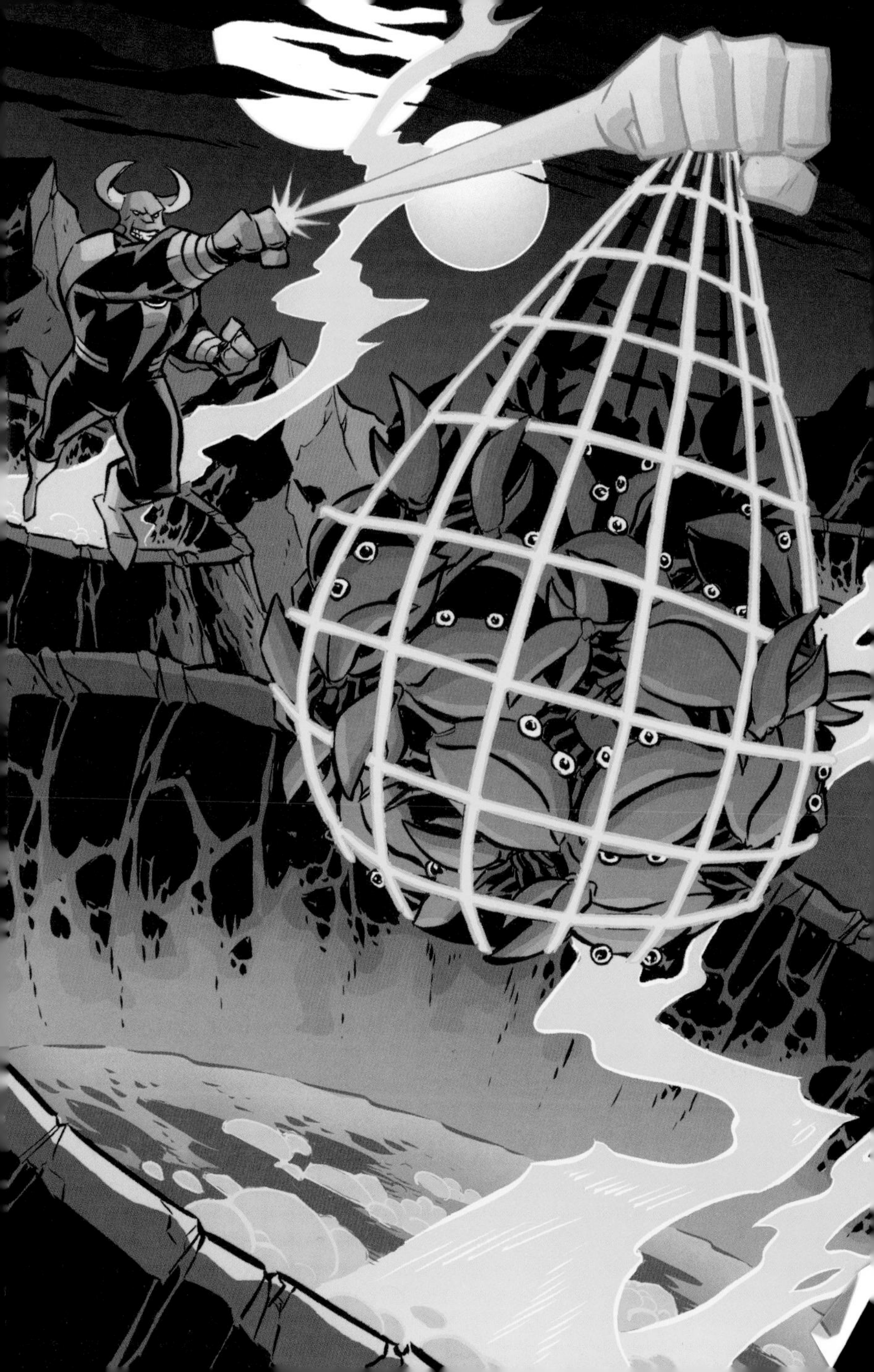

Back at the Ring of Fear, Sinestro watched a few more connectors light up. It still wasn't enough to satisfy him.

"Maybe Sirket is doing better," Sinestro said. "Sirket, report!"

"I put a web . . . clikkk-clikkk . . . around Apiaton now," Sirket said. "It's very tight . . . clikkk-clikkk. They can no longer move, and soon they'll no longer breathe. The fly people are very scared."

"More, Sirket, more!" Sinestro ordered. Then he contacted another Corps member. "Maash, report!"

"We're in Sector 1416," Maash answered. Actually, it was one of his faces that spoke. He had three of them.

"We ran into the Green Lantern named Chaselon," another face said.

"We almost cracked his big crystal skull," the third face reported.

"We're attacking a triple star system now," the first face said.

Sinestro watched the Ring of Fear light up. The globes were energizing faster and faster now. The Sinestro Corps was doing its job spreading terror and panic. Soon, the Ring of Fear would be fully charged and Qward could be transported

"It won't be long before I rule this universe," Sinestro said.

CLANK! A green cage formed around Sinestro like a prison cell. Thick green chains wrapped around his body.

"The universe is getting along just fine without you, Sinestro," said Hal Jordan. A beam from his power ring formed the cage.

"You should get a hobby," Brokk suggested. His power ring formed the chains.

"You can't stop what's happening," Sinestro told them. "My Ring of Fear is about to change this universe."

Hal looked at the string of glowing globes. It curved far out of sight. "Ring, analyze those objects," he commanded.

"They are components of a Qwa-Portal of extreme size," the power ring answered. Not only was the ring a formidable weapon, it was also a powerful computer.

"Why so big?" Brokk asked.

"Because he plans to teleport something big," Hal realized.

"By the time you figure it out, it'll be too late," Sinestro gloated.

"Not if we destroy it first," Hal said.

The two Green Lanterns fired beams of intense green energy at the nearest globes. Nothing happened.

"Your green rings won't hurt the Ring of Fear," Sinestro said with a laugh. "And your green energy can't hold me, either."

There was a flash of bright yellow light. When it faded, Sinestro was free. His yellow power ring glowed. He was ready for a fight. The Green Lanterns did not disappoint him.

Hal formed an armored tank with his ring. Brokk created a ramming beast from his homeworld.

They smashed Sinestro between them.

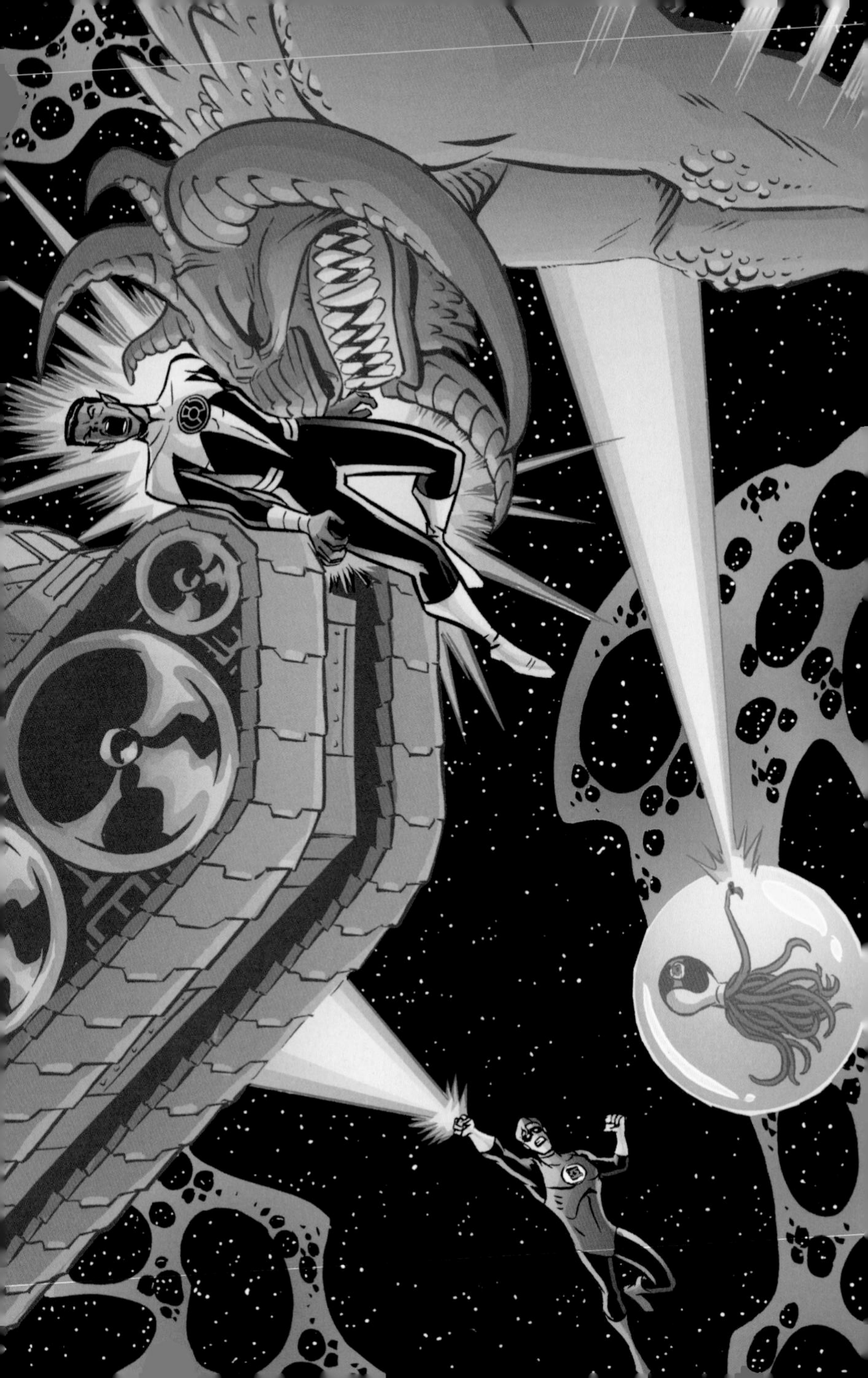

Sinestro pulled the creations apart with yellow energy claws. Then Brokk tried to wrap Sinestro in a cocoon of green energy, but the super-villain cut it with yellow scissors. Hal tried to knock out Sinestro with a giant green boxing glove. Sinestro deflected it with an even bigger metal fist.

The battle with Sinestro was keeping Hal and Brokk from stopping the Ring of Fear

"It's time to call in reinforcements," Hal said. He commanded his ring to send out an emergency broadcast. "Attention Green Lantern Corps! Urgent alert in Sector 0981."

Sinestro showed no fear. He smiled his evil smile instead. He commanded his power ring to make a similar broadcast. "Attention Sinestro Corps!" he said. "Return to the Ring of Fear. The Green Lanterns are coming!"

CHAPTER 5

COUNTDOWN

Meanwhile, the Thunderers and Weaponers of Qward waited for their planet to be transported to the other universe. They waited for a command from their Highlord, Sinestro.

Sinestro, however, was busy. One hundred Sinestro Corps members faced an equal number of Green Lanterns at the Ring of Fear.

"Are you afraid, Hal Jordan?" Sinestro sneered. "You should be. When the Ring is complete, your universe will fall to me."

"I'm not afraid," Hal replied. "You're always trying to take over the universe. Can't you come up with a new scheme?"

Sinestro lashed out with a beam of yellow energy from his ring. The Sinestro Corps took it as a signal to attack.

Green and yellow power rings shot at each other. The darkness of space lit up with explosions of emerald and gold. Green Lanterns battled yellow Sinestros. The winners would either save, or enslave, the universe.

"You might not be afraid of me, Jordan," Sinestro shouted. "But you will be when Qward comes through that portal."

"You're transporting the whole planet?" Hal said.

"Weaponers and Thunderers of Qward are waiting to conquer your universe," Sinestro said.

Hal saw more and more globes light up. They energized one by one like seconds ticking on a clock. He knew it was a countdown to doom.

"You can't stop it," Sinestro gloated. "Surrender now."

"Never," Hal said. He turned to his comrades. "Destroy the portal at all costs!"

Suddenly, the battle shifted away from the Sinestro Corps. All the Green Lanterns turned toward the Ring of Fear. They blasted it with intense green ring energies. The string of globes flared. They were surrounded by emerald fire, but they did not burn up.

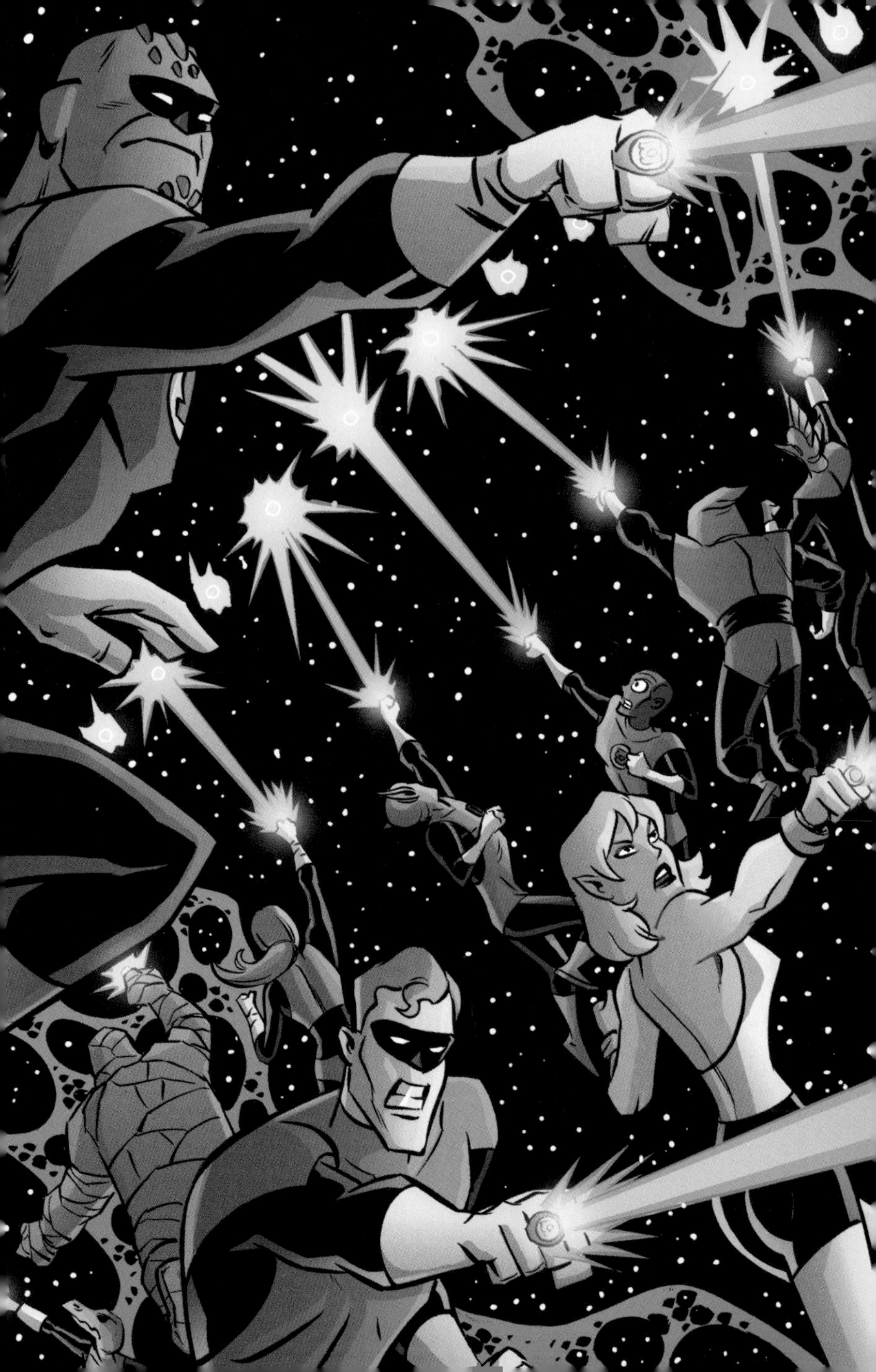

Sinestro laughed. "Get ready to call me your Highlord," he said.

Only a few more globes remained before the circuit was complete. Once those powered up, the invasion would begin.

Sinestro looked for Hal Jordan, but he was gone. "The great Hal Jordan of Earth has run away — scared!" Sinestro said. "The coward has seen the color of fear!"

"No!" Brokk shouted. "The Green Lantern Corps has sworn to protect the universe from evil's might. It is our duty."

Brokk made a desperate move. He flew between two of the globes. He hoped his body would break the circuit of power.

BOOM! There was a tremendous explosion. The force of the blast threw Brokk far away from the Ring of Fear.

The last globe lit up. The Ring of Fear was complete.

"Behold the power of Sinestro! Behold the power of fear!" Sinestro proclaimed.

A yellow energy sphere the size of a planet started to form. Sinestro could see Qward coming into focus.

An asteroid whizzed past Sinestro's head. He turned and saw Hal Jordan.

"Throwing rocks at me won't stop my invasion," Sinestro said with a laugh.

"Who said I was throwing them at *you*?" Hal replied.

Hal used his ring to push a giant swarm of asteroids toward the Ring of Fear. The big space rocks decimated the little metal spheres. The power circuit was broken.

The Qwa-Portal collapsed. The yellow energy sphere dissolved. Qward stayed in its own universe.

"Noooo!" Sinestro screamed.

The Sinestro Corps scattered as soon as they saw defeat. The Green Lanterns pursued them. Hal Jordan faced Sinestro.

"You're finished again," Hal told his foe.

"Never!" Sinestro said.

Sinestro touched his power ring's special escape program. He disappeared in a flash of yellow light. Sinestro reappeared in the empty Throne Room on Qward. It was where everything had started. He looked at the throne. It was ruined — just like his plans for conquest and revenge.

Slowly, grimly Sinestro used his power ring to rebuild it.

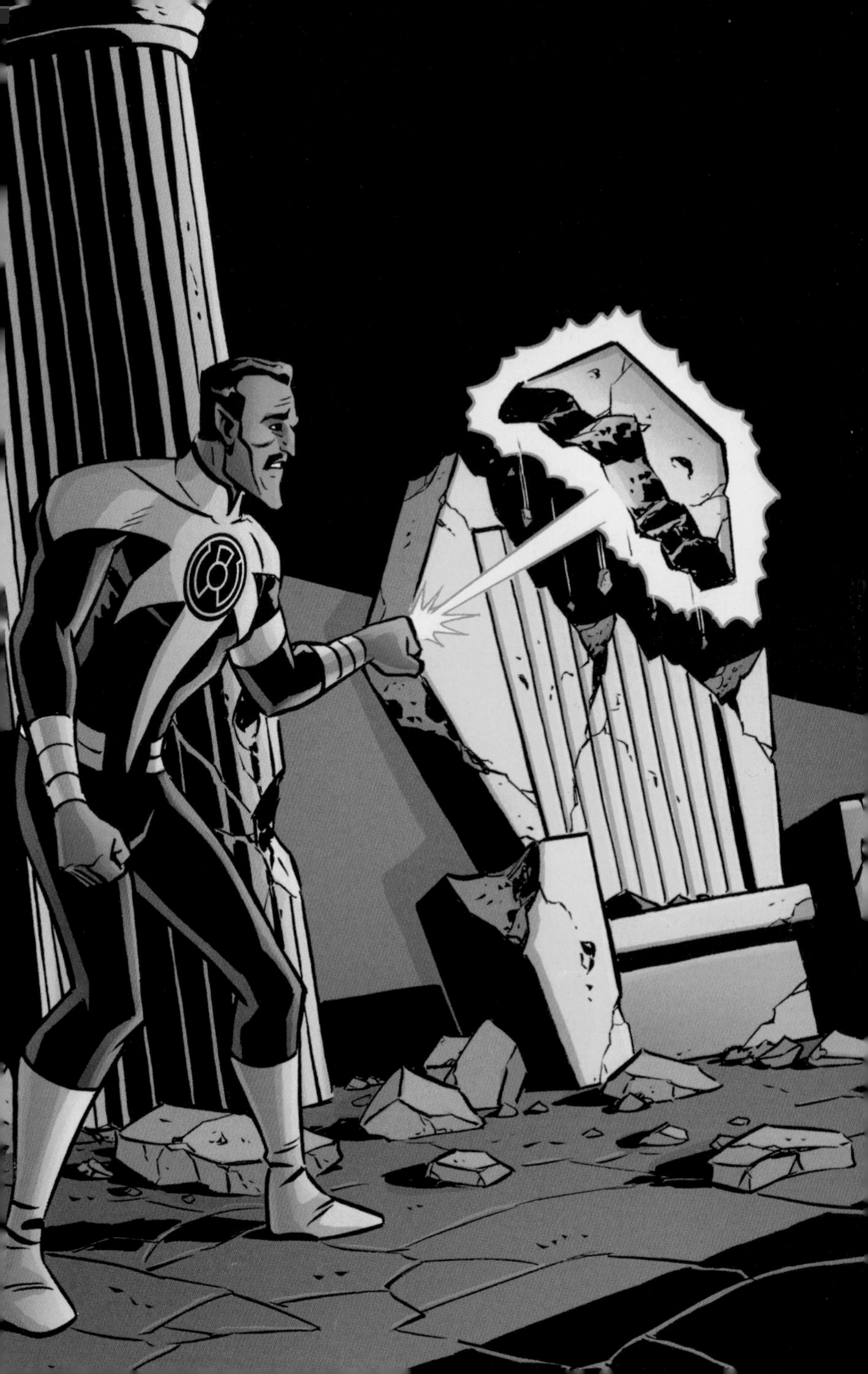

BIOGRAPHIES

Laurie S. Sutton has read comics since she was a kid. She grew up to become an editor for Marvel, DC Comics, Starblaze, and Tekno Comics. She has written *Adam Strange* for DC, *Star Trek: Voyager* for Marvel, plus *Star Trek: Deep Space Nine* and *Witch Hunter* for Malibu Comics. There are long boxes of comics in her closet where there should be clothing and shoes. Laurie has lived all over the world, and currently resides in Florida.

Shawn McManus has been drawing pictures ever since he was able to hold a pencil in his tiny little hand. Since then, he has illustrated comic books including Sandman, Batman, Dr. Fate, Spider-Man, and many others. Shawn has also done work for film, animation, and online entertainment. He lives in New England, and he loves the spring season there.

Lee Loughridge has been working in comics for more than eighteen years. He currently lives in sunny California in a tent on the beach.

GLOSSARY

allies (AL-eyez)—friends or factions that support each other or a shared cause

banish (BAN-ish)—send someone away from a place and order the person not to return

conquer (KONG-kur)—to defeat and take control of an enemy

decimated (DESS-uh-may-tid)—destroyed a great number or proportion of something

invasion (in-VAY-zhun)—the act of invading, or sending armed forces to take over and control something or someone

mayhem (MAY-hem)—a situation of confusion or violent destruction

reigns (RAYNZ)—rules as a king or queen

quiver (KWIV-ur)—a case of arrows

savage (SAV-ij)—fierce, dangerous, uncivilized, or violent

supreme (suh-PREEM)—greatest, best, or most powerful

DISCUSSION QUESTIONS

1. There are several Yellow and Green Lanterns in this story. Which one is your favorite? Why?

2. What makes Sinestro a villain? What makes Hal Jordan and Brokk heroes? Discuss your answers.

3. This book has ten illustrations. Which one is your favorite?

WRITING PROMPTS

1. A Yellow Lantern's powers are fueled by fear. Green Lanterns get their strength from willpower. If you were a Lantern, what color would you want to be? What emotion or force would you use as fuel? Write about yourself as a Lantern, then draw a picture of yourself wearing your Lantern uniform.

2. Green Lanterns fight for good. Yellow Lanterns fight for evil. Do you believe in good and evil? Why or why not?

3. What happens to Sinestro after this story ends? Write another chapter to this book from Sinestro's perspective. How does he feel? What are his plans? Write about it.

FUN DOESN'T STOP HERE!

DISCOVER MORE AT...

www.CAPSTONEKIDS.com

GAMES & PUZZLES

VIDEOS & CONTESTS

HEROES & VILLAINS

AUTHORS & ILLUSTRATORS

FIND COOL WEBSITES AND MORE BOOKS LIKE THIS ONE AT WWW.FACTHOUND.COM.

JUST TYPE IN THE BOOK ID:
9781434237989
AND YOU'RE READY TO GO!

LOOK FOR MORE

SUPER DC HEROES
VILLAINS

LEX LUTHOR AND THE
KRYPTONITE CAVERNS

JOKER ON THE
HIGH SEAS

CHEETAH AND THE
PURRFECT CRIME

BLACK MANTA AND THE
OCTOPUS ARMY